THE RAREST DINOSAUR IN THE WORLD

by Miles Kington

There was once a rare breeds farm in the West of England, which only kept rare kinds of animal.

It had goats with very curly hair.

It had pigs with spots all over.

It had sheep with horns that went round and round, like corkscrews.

It had Scottish cows which were so hairy, they could hardly see out of their eyes or hear out of their ears.

Even the tractors were quite rare. There was one tractor that had grass growing out of its wheels. This was because the tractor couldn't go, so the children climbed all over it, which some children thought was more fun than looking at rare animals.

There was also a farmer on the farm who looked after all the rare breeds. The farmer had very curly hair, and some spots, but she wasn't a rare breed.

One day a boy went up to the farmer and said: "Do you have any dinosaurs on the farm!"

"No," said the farmer.

"Well, a dinosaur is a rare breed," said the boy.

"No, he isn't," said the farmer. "He is an extinct breed. There are no more dinosaurs. They all died millions of years ago."

"How do you know?" said the boy.

"Because it says so in books," said the farmer.

Well, the farmer had been reading the wrong books, because there was one dinosaur left. He was called Dai, which sounds Welsh, but is just short for dinosaur.

At the time when the dinosaurs all died out, about a hundred million years ago, Dai happened to be away on holiday.

When he got back all the other dinosaurs had died out, and he was the only one left, and it wasn't the same without the other dinosaurs.

For one thing, he was lonely without another dinosaur to talk to, and for another thing, the earth had now been taken over by human beings, who were very noisy and fought a lot.

So the dinosaur decided to hide.

You might think it was very difficult for a dinosaur to hide, as he is so big he cannot hide behind anything, but there are more ways of hiding than getting behind something.

You can pretend to be something else. A small hill, perhaps, or a large leisure centre which is not yet open to the public.

For millions of years he hid during the day, and looked for food at night, when nobody else was awake.

For his holidays he used to go to Loch Ness and some people, who have seen him going for a dip, call him the Loch Ness monster, perhaps because of the horrible purple bathing costume he sometimes wears.

But one day, when he was in the West Country, he heard of a rare breeds farm that had only rare breeds. He was pretending to be a hill, and two crows landed on him and started to chat about the farm.

"Have you been to the rare breeds farm, then?"

"Why would I want to go to a rare breeds farm?"

"To learn something."

"Why would I want to learn something?"

"Because you are so stupid."

"Why am I so stupid?"

As you can see, crows talk about pretty silly things when they get together, but the dinosaur thought the rare breeds farm sounded very interesting. Perhaps they would be interested in having a dinosaur.

He said: "Yes, interesting," to himself.

"Did you hear that?" said one crow.

"Did I hear what?"

"Did you hear the hill say something?"

"What did the hill say?"

"It said: "Yes, interesting.""

"What's interesting?"

"I don't know. Ask the hill."

"But if I ask the hill questions, you will say I'm stupid."

"But you are stupid anyway..."

Never listen to a crow's conversation, unless you are a dinosaur pretending to be a hill, and have to, while you're very still.

As soon as the two crows flew away, and it was night, the dinosaur started looking for the rare breeds farm. It took him two years, but when you're two hundred million years old, that's not very long. Finally, he found it.

He waited until it was dark, then went very slowly up to the farmhouse.

"That's funny," said the farmer, looking out of her window, into the night.

"What's funny?" said her husband.

"Well, we used to have a big lawn outside the front door. Now we have a big hill."

"No," said her husband, looking hard, "I think it's a big marquee. Are we having a wedding tomorrow?"

"I don't think so," said the farmer. "Anyway, marquees don't have heads. Look, this one has got a head."

She said this as the dinosaur very slowly moved his head to the front door and knocked on it with his nose. The farmer opened the door.

"I'm afraid the rare breeds farm is closed for the night," she said, feeling a bit scared. "Could you come back in a hundred years time?"

"Do you want a dinosaur in your farm?" said Dai the dinosaur. "I'm very rare."

"How rare?" said the farmer.

"Very rare. I'm the only one left."

He told the farmer his story, and said he had been looking for somewhere to live for about two million years.

"Have you tried many places?" said the farmer.

"No," said Dai the dinosaur. "This is the first place I've tried. But I think I would be a great success on a rare breeds farm. People would come from miles away to see me."

"Yes," said the farmer, "but what if you eat all the other animals? Or sit on them by mistake? Or eat me?"

"That's silly. Dinosaurs don't eat animals. They only eat grass, vegetables and interesting salads."

"I'll just look it up in my book to make sure," said the farmer, and she went to look it up in a book called *Dinosaurs: What they eat*, then in another book called *The Dinosaur Diet Book* and another one called *When Dinosaurs Ruled The Restaurants Of The World*.

He was right.

They only ate green stuff.

It sounded boring to the farmer, but she was glad of it.

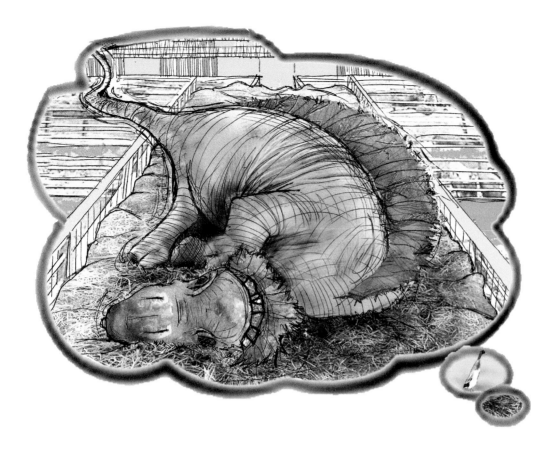

"I could be very useful round the farm," said the Dinosaur, "I could squash silage flat, just as well as a pile of old tractor tyres.

I could roll fields that needed rolling. I could pull trees away after they had blown down in the storms. I could be a bouncy castle..."

"A What?" said the farmer.

" You know – those things they have at fairgrounds, and open days at grand houses, where the children get in and bounce up and down.

I could lie on my back and stick my legs up in the air to pretend to be the four towers of the castle, then the children could climb on my stomach and..."

"All right, all right, all right," said the farmer. "But what will you do if I say you can't come here?"

"I will have to go away and live by myself in the mountains again," said Dai the dinosaur, sniffing horribly. A tear ran down his cheek and fell on the lawn, making a small pond.

"All right," said the farmer. "You can stay in the field behind

the woods and come out when the farm has an Open Day
to see what the public thinks."

"They'll love me!"

"They might be scared stiff," sighed the farmer.

The Open Day came nearer and nearer. The dinosaur practised not frightening people.

And then one day a terrible thing happened. Dai the dinosaur became very ill, and the farmer didn't have any books about dinosaur diseases or how to give a prehistoric animal pills.

So she sent for the vet.

"Ever seen a dinosaur?" she asked the vet.

"Dinosaurs are extinct," said the vet. "They died out millions of years ago..."

"That's what I thought," said the farmer. "See that hill over there...?"

The vet, who had never seen a dinosaur before, very bravely gave the animal a complete examination and then came back to the farmer.

"There are two things wrong with your dinosaur," he said. "One, he has a slight cold. Two, he's going to have a baby. It isn't a he, it's a she."

The vet was absolutely right. That was why the dinosaur was feeling a bit ill.

So they stopped calling him Dai, and started calling her Di, which is after all the same name, and instead of letting everyone climb over her at the Open Day, they had to keep her quiet, waiting for the baby to come.

"Next year you can go out in the farm, together with your baby," they told her.

"But this year you will have to keep out of the way."

If you look carefully behind the farm, behind the field, behind the woods, you might see a green hill, which is really a dinosaur pretending to be a hill. If there are two crows on it, that proves it. The conversation between the two crows goes something like this...

"I've been on this hill before."

"What do you mean you've been on this hill before?"

"This hill. I've been on it. Before."

"It's very easy to go on a hill again, if you've been on it before."

"But last time the hill was somewhere else."

"What do you mean, this hill was somewhere else?"

"This hill has moved."

"Hills don't move."

"This one has..."

And so on, and so forth. Silly, isn't it?

Anyway, don't forget to come back next year and see the dinosaur, complete with baby.